Bellossom's Big Battle

**Pokémon junior**

**There are more books about Pokémon for younger readers.**

Bellossom's Big Battle

POKÉMON junior

#11

Adapted by S. E. Heller

SCHOLASTIC INC.
New York  Toronto  London  Auckland  Sydney
Mexico City  New Delhi  Hong Kong

ISBN 0-439-23400-X

Designed by Carisa Swenson

12  11  10  9  8  7  6                    7 8 9 10/0

Printed in the U.S.A.

First Scholastic printing, July 2001

# CHAPTER ONE

## Show Town

Pikachu and its friends were traveling. They came to a big city. It was called Florando. Pikachu and its trainer, Ash Ketchum, were excited to explore. Misty and her Pokémon Togepi were hungry for hamburgers. And their friend Brock wanted to meet girls.

Pikachu, Ash, Misty, Togepi, and Brock traveled everywhere together. Ash was on a mission to become the world's greatest Pokémon trainer! Pikachu and the others wanted to help him.

Soon the friends came to a busy street. A girl was handing out flyers. Pikachu was excited to hear about a Pokémon talent competition.

"Florando is famous for its per-formances," said Brock.

It was true. Pikachu had never seen so many amazing Pokémon.

A Fire Pokémon jumped through a hoop of fire. Oddish, a small Weed Pokémon, was balancing on Electrode, a Pokémon shaped like a ball. Alakazam, a Psychic Pokémon, was using its mental powers to bend objects. Lots of Water Pokémon, like Wartortle,

Psyduck, and Poliwhirl had created a beautiful fountain.

"Wow!" said Ash.

*"Pika pika!"* cheered Pikachu.

Then Ash pointed to two small
Pokémon. They had flowers on
their heads and they seemed to
be dancing in the air. Pikachu had
never seen anything like them.
Who were they?

# CHAPTER TWO

## Dancing Pokémon

Ash checked Dexter, his Pokédex. The screen showed a picture of Bellossom, the Flower Pokémon. Dexter said:

"These Pokémon are dancers. As they walk, their delicate petals rub together, making a lovely sound."

"They really move!" said Brock.

*"Brrr!"* agreed Togepi.

The Bellossom's trainer called
out a new move. It was a loop-de-
loop. One Flower Pokémon lifted
the other. The Bellossom went
tumbling through the air! It
flipped in a
beautiful
somersault.
But then, it
lost control!
With a
thump, the
Bellossom
landed in
Ash's arms.

*"Pika!"* cried Pikachu as they all fell down.

Worried, the Bellossom's trainer ran over. She was grateful to Ash for catching her Pokémon. To thank him, she offered the friends some cold drinks.

"I am Bailey," said the Bellossom's trainer. "These are my star dancers, Belle and Bella."

Pikachu and Togepi were happy to meet the Flower Pokémon.

"Will your dance team be in the competition tomorrow?" Ash asked Bailey. She nodded, but

Belle looked sad.

"What is the matter?" Misty asked the little Flower Pokémon.

Bailey explained that the Bellossom were having trouble with the Bell-loop-de-loop trick. Smiling at Belle, Bailey tried to comfort her Pokémon.

"There is still time," Bailey said. "Hang in there, Belle."

# CHAPTER THREE

## Meowth Onstage

Not far down the road, Team Rocket had also entered Florando. Jessie, James, and their talking Pokémon, Meowth, were following Ash and Pikachu and their friends. Team Rocket wanted to steal Pikachu for their boss, Giovanni. Giovanni collected rare Pokémon.

"Look where we are!" cried James.

"A street performance," replied Meowth.

"Now's our chance!" said Jessie.

"If we cannot earn a buck here, where can we?" asked James.

"Make money? How?" asked Meowth.

"By performing in the street, of course," Jessie answered.

"But doing what?" asked Meowth.

"Leave it to me. Come see the rarest Pokémon . . . talking

Meowth!" Jessie called to the crowd.

Meowth was surprised. "Who, me?"

Jessie pulled Meowth onto a stage. People gathered around to see it talk. But Meowth had stage fright. Its knees started to shake.

"Just talk!" ordered Jessie.

*"Meowth,"* gulped Meowth.

"Say something!" ordered James, but Meowth did not know what to say. It wanted a script.

Jessie and James gave Meowth jokes to tell. They were not very

funny. Meowth mixed up the words. Jessie and James laughed, but no else did. Soon the crowd began to walk away. Jessie and James tried to collect money, but no coins filled their cans.

Everyone thought Meowth's

human talk was a trick. They thought Jessie and James were the ones talking for Meowth. Soon the crowd disappeared.

Jessie and James were not discouraged. They decided to get a bigger stage. Jessie wanted to dance. James wanted to be a ballerina.

"Soon we will be rich!" cried Jessie.

Meowth was not so sure.

# CHAPTER FOUR

## Showdown

Pikachu was not happy to see Team Rocket. They were always up to no good. Now Jessie, James, and Meowth plowed down a busy street with a bulldozer. Jessie and James were on top of it. They were dressed as dancers.

"Be careful!" yelled Ash. He

stepped in front of the bulldozer to make it stop.

Team Rocket was not happy that Ash put an end to their show. They called for a battle.

"Go, Pikachu!" cried Ash.

*"Pika!"* cried the yellow Pokémon. It rose in the air to attack, but Bailey stopped it. Pikachu was surprised.

"This place is important to me and my Bellossom," she said. "We would like to protect it."

Other performers wanted to help, too. Alakazam turned the

bulldozer upside down with its psychic powers. Team Rocket fell to the ground.

Now Jessie called Arbok, her Poison Pokémon. James called Victreebel, a giant Pokémon.

"Bella, Belle, go!" called Bailey. The little Flower Pokémon danced around Arbok's Poison Sting. They dodged

Victreebel with Back Step Turn.

"*Pika!*" cheered Pikachu. Its

friends were

doing a

great job.

"Stop them by

attacking at the same

time!" yelled Meowth.

Jessie and James called for

Wrap Attack. Arbok and Victreebel

moved toward the two Bellossom.

"Jumping Turn!" cried Bailey. As

Bella and Belle jumped in the air,

Victreebel and Arbok crashed

together.

When Bailey told the Bellossom
to use Sleep Powder, Victreebel
and Arbok fell asleep.

"You will not get
away with this!" Team
Rocket cried as they
ran away.

Belle and Bella
smiled happily. The crowd
cheered for the Bellossom.

"That was Bellossom's battle
dancing," said Bailey. The dance
team bowed. Everyone clapped
for the wonderful show.

"Everything is a performance

here," said Misty.

"But winning a battle with dancing—that is great," Brock said.

"Yeah, it really is battle dancing!" cried Ash.

# CHAPTER FIVE

## Dancing Dreams

That night Pikachu, Togepi,
Belle, and Bella played together.
Pikachu liked its new friends.
They were teaching it to dance.
And it was fun to dance with the
Flower Pokémon.

Ash asked Bailey how she had

decided to train her Bellossom to dance.

"I learned dance to help with battle training," Bailey explained. "Then, when I started working with Bellossom I had a change of heart. Creating the world's best Pokémon dance team became my goal."

*"Ahn, ahn."* The Bellossom smiled, nodding. That was their dream, too.

Bailey explained that dance was a lot like battle. The steps and rhythm needed for both were almost the same. Belle and Bella were strong like many fighters, but they were graceful, too.

"Still, if we want to be the best at dance, we have to do the Bell-loop-de-loop trick perfectly," said Bailey.

Belle and Bella agreed. They wanted to try again.

# CHAPTER SIX

## Dance Practice

The next morning Pikachu joined the two Bellossom for practice. Bailey called out steps as the Pokémon danced. It was hard work, but Pikachu loved it!

*"Pika pi!"* said the Pokémon happily. It was having fun!

"You are doing great, Pikachu!"

cheered Ash. He clapped his hands.

"*Ahn, ahn.*" The Bellossom nodded.

Even Bailey agreed. She told Pikachu how to use the moves during an attack.

"*Pikachu!*" These dance steps would be helpful in battle.

Now it was the Bellossom's turn to practice a Bell-loop-de-loop.

"Jump as hard as you can," Bailey told Belle.

When Bailey gave the signal, Belle ran to Bella. Bella gave Belle a boost in the air. Pikachu watched its friend soar.

"*Pika!*" cheered Pikachu.

Belle was doing great. Then the Flower Pokémon became scared. Belle was remembering the last time it fell. Now Belle could not control the move anymore. It tumbled to the ground.

"It is okay, Belle," said Bailey. "You did your best."

Still, the Bellossom were unhappy. They would not be able to do a Bell-loop-de-loop in the competition.

# CHAPTER SEVEN

## Team Rocket Steals the Show

It was showtime. The Pokémon performers lined the stage.

"Good luck," Ash called to Bailey.

*"Pika!"* Pikachu called to the Bellossom.

The crowd cheered for all the Pokémon. The two Bellossom were

"Ready, Pikachu?" asked Ash.

*"Pikachu!"* The Pokémon nodded. It climbed onto Heracross's horn. Pikachu was determined to save its friends.

"Go, Heracross!" cried Ash.

With a powerful motion, Heracross tossed Pikachu into the sky. The yellow Pokémon flew like a rocket. It grabbed hold of the balloon.

"Pikachu, Thunderbolt!" shouted Ash.

*"PIKACHUUU!"*

The balloon lit up with Pikachu's electricity. It burst!

"Pikachu!" cried Ash as the balloon crashed.

Pikachu crawled out, unharmed. It jumped into Ash's arms. The other Pokémon were okay, too. But they were still trapped in the net.

Ash was happy that his Pokémon was not hurt. And he was proud of Pikachu for being so brave.

# CHAPTER EIGHT

## Pikachu's Battle Dance

Together, Pikachu and Ash faced Team Rocket.

"Give back the Pokémon you stole!" shouted Ash.

"I do not think so," said Jessie. She called Arbok. James called Victreebel.

"Go, Pikachu!" said Ash.

Jessie called for Poison Sting Attack. Arbok opened its mouth. Pikachu remembered what Bellossom had done yesterday. As Ash called out dance steps, the Pikachu easily danced around the attack.

"Victreebel! Take Down!" called James.

Now the Pokémon came after Pikachu. It slammed its strong leaves.

"Pikachu! Backstep," called Ash.

Pikachu stepped away quickly,

and Victreebel could not get the little yellow Pokémon.

"Attack from both sides," Jessie told Arbok and Victreebel. "Flank with Tackle!"

Now Arbok and Victreebel surrounded Pikachu. They lunged forward. Just before they reached Pikachu, Ash told his Pokémon to jump. Arbok and Victreebel crashed together!

Pikachu flew through the air. It thought that it had escaped. But Team Rocket did not give up.

"Victreebel, Wrap!" cried James.

The Plant Pokémon wrapped a vine around Pikachu. The yellow Pokémon could not get away.

"Arbok, use Bite," called Jessie quickly. "Attack from above!"

As the Pokémon came close, Pikachu cried out. It needed help!

# CHAPTER NINE

## Bell-loop-de-loop

Bailey knew what to do. When Jessie and James were not looking, she lifted the net. The two Bellossom wanted to help Pikachu.

"Hurry!" said Bailey.

Belle ran toward Bella. Bella tossed its partner high in the air.

Belle was turning in circles. The little Pokémon opened its eyes. It began to get nervous. Then Belle thought of Pikachu. The Flower Pokémon concentrated. It moved with great control.

Arbok was about to bite Pikachu. Just in time, Belle sailed toward the Pokémon. It hit Arbok hard, knocking it down.

Bailey was so proud of her Pokémon. "You did a Bell-loop-de-loop!" she cried.

"Pikachu, Thunderbolt!" called Ash.

Now electricity blasted
Victreebel.

It was time to send Team Rocket
flying. Spinning at triple speed, the
two Bellossom created a tornado.
They circled Team Rocket. Around
and around went Jessie, James,

and Meowth. The tornado sent them away!

"Looks like Team Rocket is blasting off again!" Jessie, James, and Meowth cried.

# CHAPTER TEN

## A Dazzling Dance

"Hooray!" cried the crowd. The trainers all hugged their Pokémon. Everyone was okay.

"You did it!" Ash called to Pikachu and the two Bellossom.

The Pokémon smiled happily.

Bailey was very proud of Belle and Bella. They had perfected the

44

Bell-loop-de-loop all by them-
selves.

━━━━━

With strength and grace, the
Flower Pokémon twirled onstage.
They floated and jumped as the
crowd watched in awe.

Finally Bailey called for a Bell-
loop-de-loop. Belle and Bella felt
confident. Bella lifted Belle at just
the right time. As the Flower
Pokémon danced through the air
beautiful petals rained down.
Music filled the stage. With joy,

Belle landed lightly.

As the dance team bowed, the crowd went wild!

"*Brrr!*" cheered Togepi.

"*Pika!*" cheered Pikachu.

Everyone clapped for a perfect

performance.

At the same time, on the other side of Florando, Jessie, James, and Meowth were still spinning.

"Somebody stop us!" cried James.

"We are getting dizzy!" Team Rocket cried together.